Dear Parent:
Your child's love of reading starts here!

Every child learns to read in a different way and at his or her own speed. Some go back and forth between reading levels and read favorite books again and again. Others read through each level in order. You can help your young reader improve and become more confident by encouraging his or her own interests and abilities. From books your child reads with you to the first books he or she reads alone, there are I Can Read Books for every stage of reading:

SHARED READING
Basic language, word repetition, and whimsical illustrations, ideal for sharing with your emergent reader

BEGINNING READING
Short sentences, familiar words, and simple concepts for children eager to read on their own

READING WITH HELP
Engaging stories, longer sentences, and language play for developing readers

READING ALONE
Complex plots, challenging vocabulary, and high-interest topics for the independent reader

ADVANCED READING
Short paragraphs, chapters, and exciting themes for the perfect bridge to chapter books

I Can Read Books have introduced children to the joy of reading since 1957. Featuring award-winning authors and illustrators and a fabulous cast of beloved characters, I Can Read Books set the standard for beginning readers.

A lifetime of discovery begins with the magical words **"I Can Read!"**

Visit www.icanread.com for information
on enriching your child's reading experience.

Rio

BLU AND FRIENDS

I Can Read Book® is a trademark of HarperCollins Publishers.

Rio: Blu and Friends
www.icanread.com
Library of Congress catalog card number: 2010941624
ISBN 978-0-06-201487-0

Typography by Rick Farley

11 12 13 14 15 LP/WOR 10 9 8 7 6 5 4 3 2 1   ❖   First Edition

Rio

BLU AND FRIENDS

Adapted by Catherine Hapka

Based on the motion picture screenplay

by Todd R. Jones and Earl Richey Jones

HARPER

An Imprint of HarperCollinsPublishers

Blu was a blue Spix's Macaw.

He lived in Minnesota

with his best friend and owner, Linda.

Blu lived indoors and didn't fly.

He hardly ever saw other birds.

But he didn't mind.

He liked his quiet life with Linda.

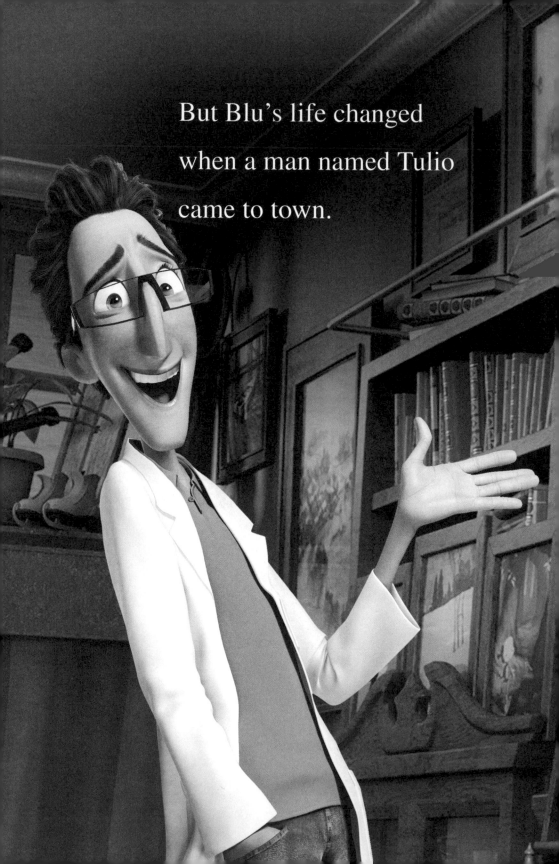

But Blu's life changed
when a man named Tulio
came to town.

Tulio told Blu that
he was the last male blue Spix's Macaw
in the entire world.
The only female blue Spix's Macaw
was at Tulio's home—in Rio!

Tulio talked Linda into taking Blu
to far-off Rio de Janeiro, Brazil.
Before Blu knew it,
they were on their way!

Rio was very different

from snowy Minnesota.

There were hot, crowded beaches

and colorful wild birds everywhere.

Tulio ran an aviary in Rio,

where he helped save rare birds.

Here, Blu met the last of his kind.

Her name was Jewel.

But Jewel didn't care about Blu.

She only cared about escaping.

Jewel felt trapped.

Someone else had heard

about Blu's arrival in Rio.

His name was Marcel.

He was a smuggler.

Marcel and his gang of thieves
tried to kidnap Blu and Jewel
to sell them.

One member of Marcel's gang
was a scruffy cockatoo named Nigel.
Nigel used to be a big TV star.
Then he was replaced
by a prettier, more colorful bird.

After that, Nigel hated pretty, colorful birds.

He helped Marcel kidnap Blu and Jewel.

Blu and Jewel managed to escape

from the smugglers.

But now they were chained together.

They needed help.

In the rain forest, they met
a friendly toucan named Rafael.
Rafael was a good talker
and an even better singer.

Blu and Jewel asked Rafael to help
free them from their chain.
Rafael knew he couldn't do it himself.

But he knew someone who could—

his friend Luiz.

The problem was

Luiz lived on the other side of Rio

and Blu did not know how to fly!

Blu had to learn to fly—

and Rafael was going to teach him.

Rafael took him to a rocky cliff.

Hang gliders took off all around them.
"If our featherless friends can do it,
how hard can it be?" Rafael said.

Blu decided he would try.

He started running,

but then he got scared.

He stopped, but Jewel didn't.

She pulled him over the edge.

They fell off the cliff.

Blu was sure this was the end!

Luckily, Blu and Jewel landed

on a passing hang glider.

Suddenly, Blu was flying.

He was really flying.

It felt amazing—until he stood up.

The wind caught his wings
and blew him off the glider.
He and Jewel landed with a thud
on the beach.

Blu, Jewel, and Rafael continued
on their way to Luiz's shop.

Blu was expecting Luiz to be a bird.

But he was wrong.

Luiz was a huge, slobbering bulldog!

Luiz had a plan to free

Blu and Jewel from their chain.

All Blu and Jewel had to do

was stay very still.

Once he was free, Blu made his way
across Rio to find Linda.

When Blu found Linda,
they both realized they had made
great new friends in Rio.
They decided to stay in Rio—
where they belonged!